DRAGONBLOOD

D1513535

DRAGON
COWBOY

BY MICHAEL DAHL

ILLUSTRATED BY
FEDERICO PIATTI

Raintree

www.raintreepublishers.co.uk
Visit our website to find out
more information about
Raintree books.

To order:
Phone 0845 6044371
Fax +44 (0) 1865 312263
Email myorders@capstonepub.co.uk

Customers from outside the UK please telephone +44 1865 312262

Raintree is an imprint of Capstone Global Library Limited,
a company incorporated in England and Wales having its
registered office at 7 Pilgrim Street, London,
EC4V 6LB – Registered company number: 6695582

Art Director: Kay Fraser
Graphic Designer: Hilary Wacholz
Production Specialist: Michelle Biedschied
Editor: Vaarunika Dharmapala
Originated by Capstone Global Library Ltd
Printed and bound in China
by South China Printing Company Ltd

ISBN 978 1 406215 23 6 (hardback)
14 13 12 11 10
10 9 8 7 6 5 4 3 2 1

ISBN 978 1 406215 37 3 (paperback)
14 13 12 11 10
10 9 8 7 6 5 4 3 2 1

British Library Cataloguing in Publication Data
A full catalogue record for this book is available
from the British Library.

CONTENTS

Introduction

A new Age of Dragons is about to begin. The powerful creatures will return to rule the world once more, but this time it will be different. This time, they will have allies who will help them. Around the world, some young humans are making a strange discovery. They are learning that they were born with dragon blood – blood that gives them amazing powers.

CHAPTER 1
STAMPEDE

In a deep valley in Wyoming, a young cowboy **rode** his horse.

The cowboy was working on a ranch for the summer.

Some cattle had **WANDERED** off that afternoon.

He thought he saw them heading **towards** the valley.

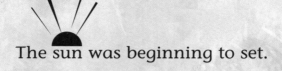 The sun was beginning to set.

Slowly, shadows 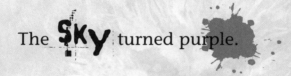 the walls on either side.

The **sky** turned purple.

The horse snorted. It was nervous.

"What's wrong, boy?" asked the cowboy. "Do you smell those cattle?"

The **missing** cattle suddenly appeared. They rushed from around the valley's **rocky** wall.

Their hooves **pounded** against the dark valley floor.

What's wrong with them? wondered the cowboy.

Then he saw a reddish light blazing behind the rocks.

A **towering** shadow appeared above the cowboy and his horse.

The shadow's 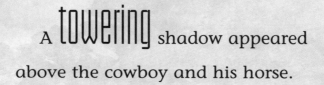 **WINGS** blotted out the stars.

FIRE ROARED from its mouth.

CHAPTER 2
THE STRANGER

The horse reared up in terror,

The cowboy GRIPPED the reins.

The shadow grew smaller.

As the cowboy watched, the shadow seemed to sink into the ground.

The boy jumped off his horse.

He **walked** over to where the shadow had vanished.

A **stranger** lay on the ground.

It was a teenage boy. **Steam** rose from his skin. A BIRTHMARK, shaped like a dragon, glowed on his arm.

CHAPTER 3
HIDING

The boy on the ground opened his eyes.

For a second, they looked like the eyes of a lizard.

Then he BLINKED, and his eyes were normal.

"I'm so cold," said the strange boy.

The cowboy **HELPED** the stranger on to his horse. Then he climbed up behind him.

An hour later, the horse reached one of the ranch's barns.

"You can stay here," said the cowboy. "No one will bother you out here."

"Thanks," said the stranger. His voice sounded weak.

As the cowboy walked towards the door, he **stopped**.

The **strange** boy was already asleep.

His dragon birthmark had stopped **glowing**.

Then the cowboy began to **scratch** his arm.

He pulled up his sleeve.

His own **BIRTHMARK** was bothering him again.

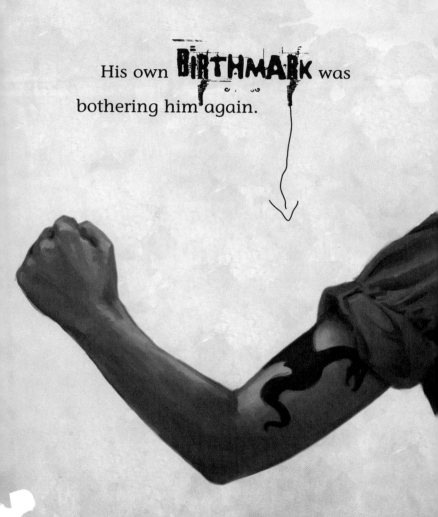

CHAPTER 4
NIGHT FLIGHT

That night, the **COWBOY** lay awake in his bed.

For many years, he had read books about dragons. The books were full of **SCALES** and wings and fire.

His father had always laughed at the books. "You're wasting your time with this rubbish," his father had told him. "You need to grow up."

That was why the cowboy was working on the **ranch** that summer. His father thought it would be good for him.

"You'll be doing real work," his father had said, "and not daydreaming about **MONSTERS.**"

The cowboy heard a noise.
He sat up and looked out of the
window at the barn.

A strange **reddish** light glowed
in its windows.

The cowboy **rushed** outside.

The strange boy was **gone**, but
the barn **wasn't** empty.

A dragon stood before him with
BLAZING eyes.

"I know it's you," said the cowboy.

The dragon **bent** its head and scratched with its claws in the dirt.

It wrote the letters: HENRY

The cowboy pulled up his sleeve and showed the dragon his **ARM**.

"Look, Henry!" he cried. "I'm the same. I'm like you. But I can't fly!"

The dragon lowered itself to the ground. He **NODDED** towards his scaly back.

The cowboy's eyes **grew** wide.

Then he quickly jumped on to the creature's back as if it were his own horse.

↑

UP and UP the monster flew.

The cowboy looked down at the ranch in the MOONLIGHT.

His father had been right. It *was* a good idea to come here.

COWBOY CLOTHING AND GEAR

In the past, a hat was an important **tool** for any cowboy. It was used as an umbrella when it rained, for shade in the hot sun, and to carry water to the cowboy's horse.

Some cowboys wore **leather** cuffs around their wrists. This would protect them from injuries. Some cowboys also wore gloves.

A cowboy would often wear a bandanna around his neck. It was called a **neckerchief**. This was a very useful tool. It could be used as a facecloth, a towel, a bandage, or a sling. It was also used to keep dust out of a cowboy's nose and mouth.

Cowboy **boots** didn't always have a pointy toe. In fact, early cowboy boots had square toes. The boots could be worn on either foot. A cowboy would have to mould them to his feet by getting them wet and walking around until they fitted.

A **vest** was another common piece of cowboy clothing. It was made of leather, canvas, or wool and used for warmth on cold nights. The pockets were very useful for storing small items like buffalo teeth and arrowheads.

Every cowboy carried a rope. In order to catch an animal, a cowboy had to learn how to throw the **ROPE** while on the ground and on his horse.

ABOUT THE AUTHOR

Michael Dahl is the author of more than 200 books for children and young adults. He has won the AEP Distinguished Achievement Award three times for his non-fiction. His Finnegan Zwake mystery series was shortlisted twice by the Anthony and Agatha awards. He has also written the Library of Doom series. He is a featured speaker at conferences on graphic novels and high-interest books for boys.

ABOUT THE ILLUSTRATOR

After getting a graphic design degree and working as a designer for a couple of years, Federico Piatti realized he was spending far too much time drawing and painting, and too much money on art books and comics, so his path took a turn towards illustration. He currently works creating imagery for books and games, mostly in the fantasy and horror genres.

GLOSSARY

birthmark mark on the skin that has been there from birth

blazing burning

blotted blocked

cattle cows, bulls, and steers that are raised for food or for their hides

creature living being

ranch large farm for cattle, sheep, or horses

reared when an animal raises itself upright on its back legs

reins straps attached to a bridle to control or guide a horse

scales small pieces of hard skin that cover the body of a reptile

valley area of low ground between two hills

DISCUSSION QUESTIONS

1. Why did the cowboy's father **send** him
to the ranch? Talk about why sometimes
parents make decisions for their kids.

2. Do you think that Henry and the cowboy
will become **friends?** Why or why not?

3. What would you do if you discovered that
you had **SECRET** powers?

WRITING PROMPTS

1. Pretend that you are **working** on a ranch for the summer. Write a letter to a friend at home about what you've done and what you've seen.

2. How did Henry get to the ranch? Write a chapter that explains how he found the cowboy.

3. At the end of this book, Henry and the cowboy are **flying.** What do you think happens next? Write about it.

MORE BOOKS TO READ

LIBRARY OF DOOM

Meet the mysterious Librarian. Keeper of the world's most dangerous books, sworn enemy of monsters made of paper and ink, crusader of young people threatened by ancient curses... Enter the Library of Doom to follow these heart-pounding adventures.